SPIDER-MAN

SPIDER-MAN

MENACE
OF THE
MOLTEN
MAN

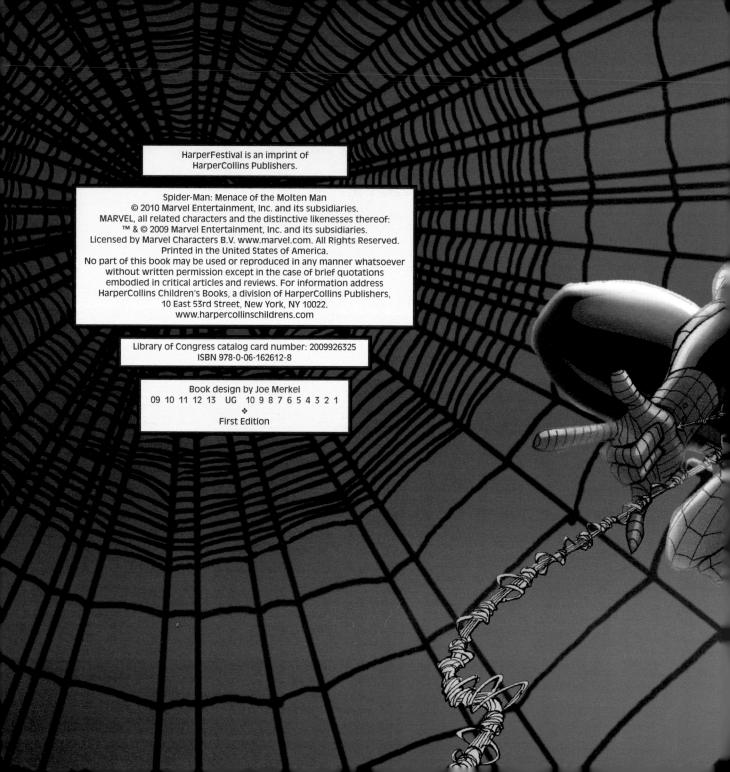

HarperFestival is an imprint of
HarperCollins Publishers.

Library of Congress catalog card number: 2009926325
ISBN 978-0-06-162612-8

Book design by Joe Merkel
09 10 11 12 13   UG   10 9 8 7 6 5 4 3 2 1
❖
First Edition

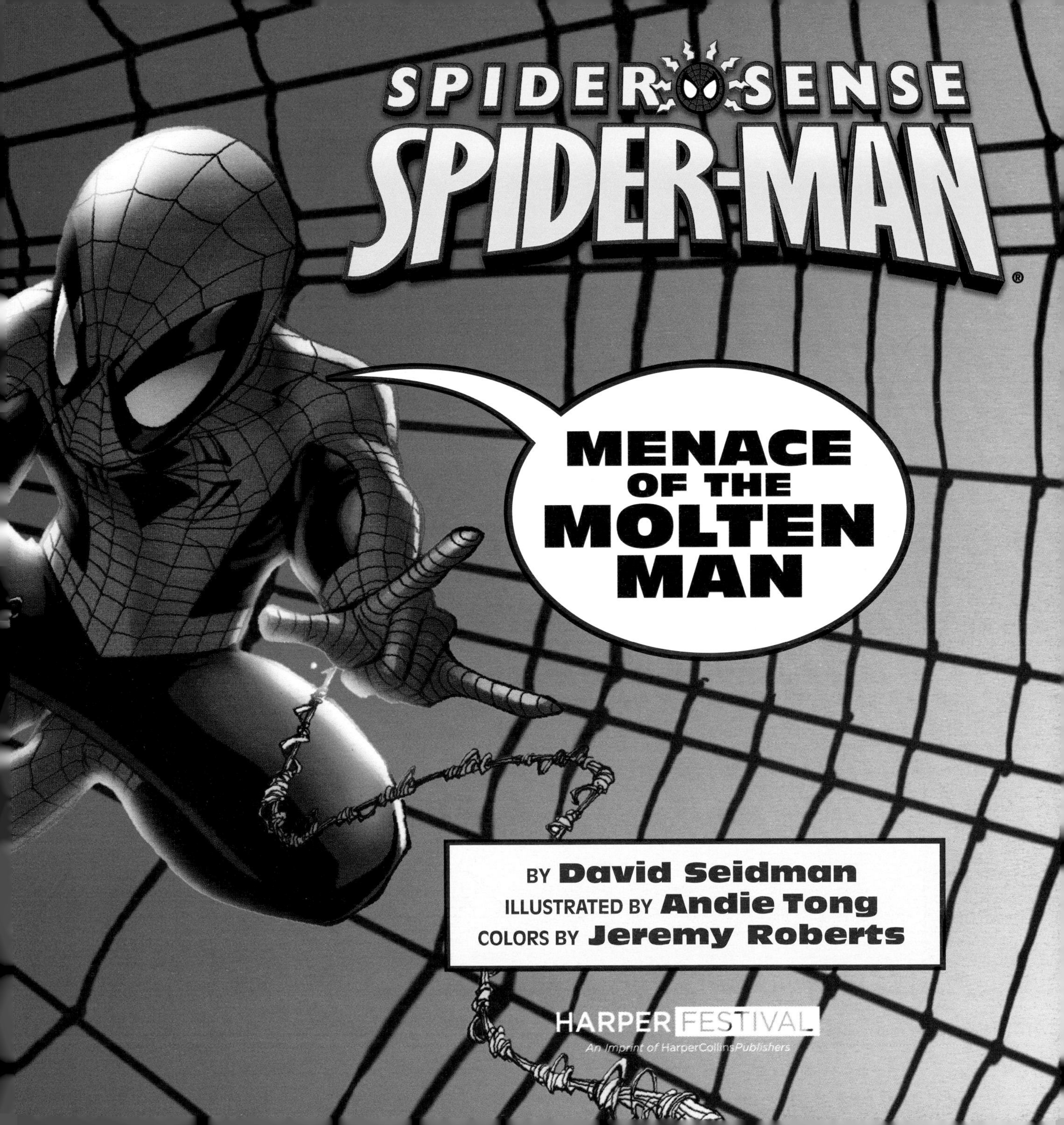

SPIDER-SENSE

SPIDER-MAN®

MENACE OF THE MOLTEN MAN

BY **David Seidman**
ILLUSTRATED BY **Andie Tong**
COLORS BY **Jeremy Roberts**

HARPER FESTIVAL
An Imprint of HarperCollinsPublishers

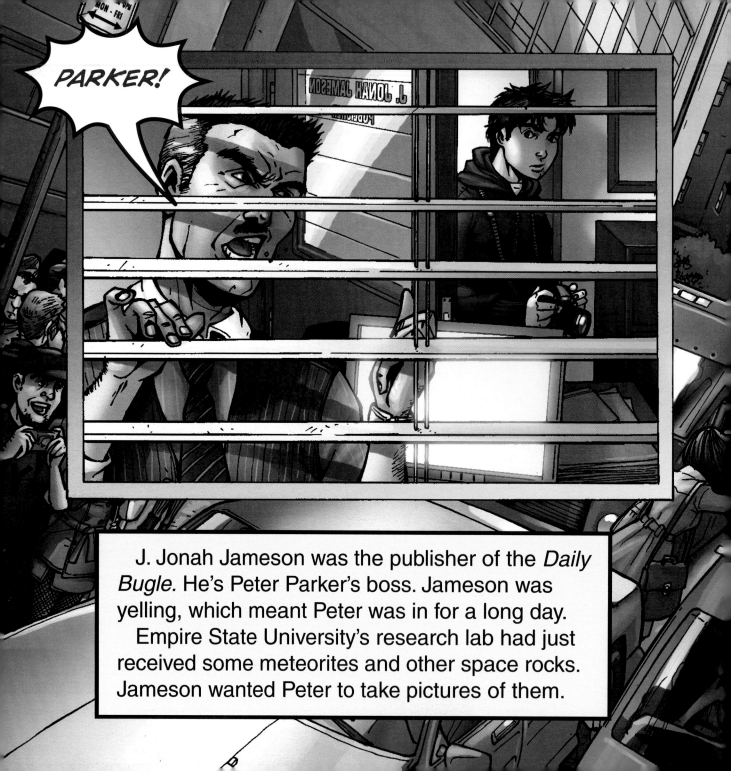

PARKER!

J. Jonah Jameson was the publisher of the *Daily Bugle.* He's Peter Parker's boss. Jameson was yelling, which meant Peter was in for a long day.

Empire State University's research lab had just received some meteorites and other space rocks. Jameson wanted Peter to take pictures of them.

So Peter headed across town the fastest way he knew how. He changed into his spider-suit and swung over the slow-moving traffic.

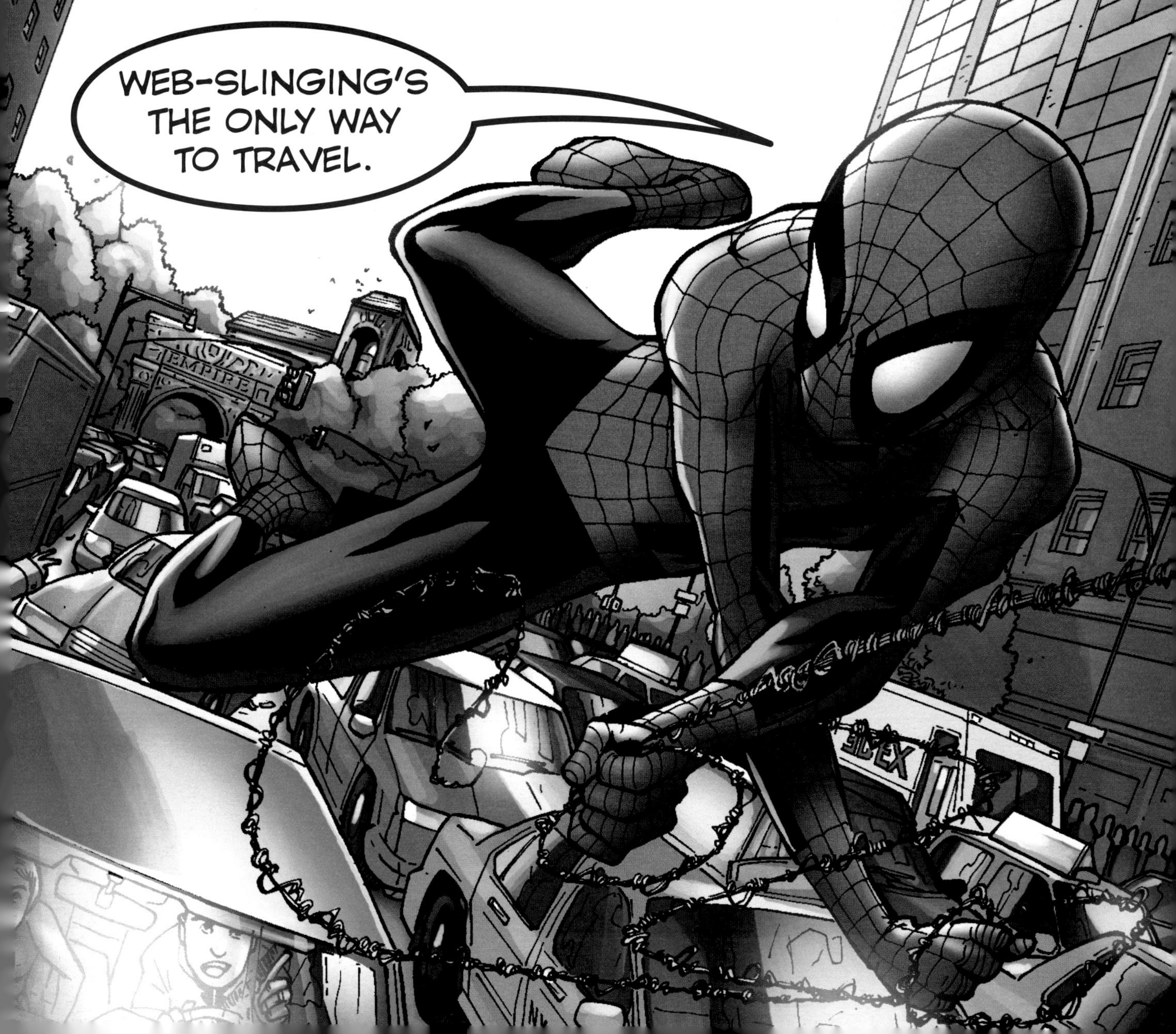
WEB-SLINGING'S THE ONLY WAY TO TRAVEL.
EMPIRE

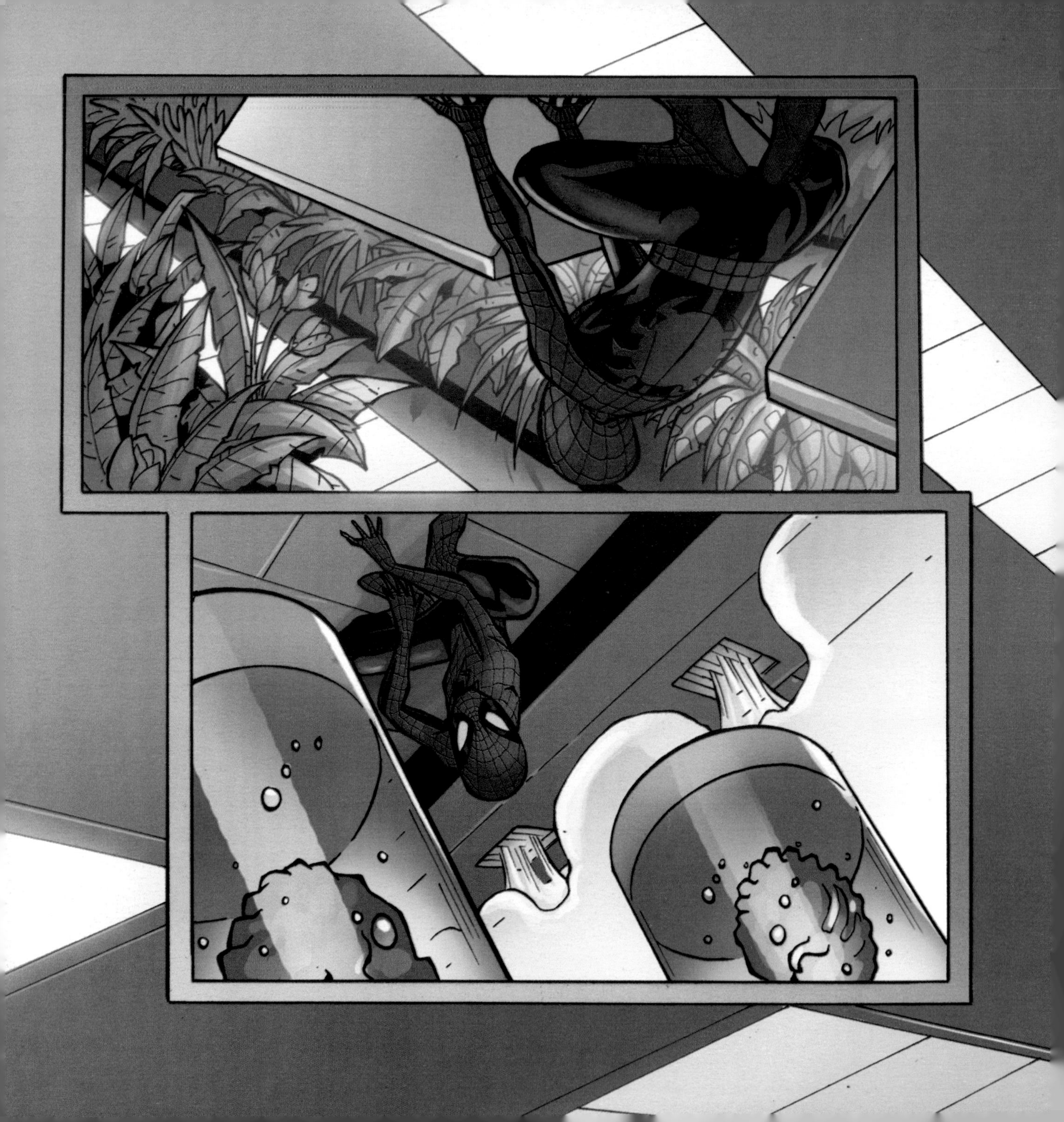

When Spider-Man arrived on the college campus, he searched everywhere for the meteorites. He crawled along the ceiling of a hothouse where strange plants grew and looked through a freezer room full of stored experiments.

Finally, he reached the research lab.

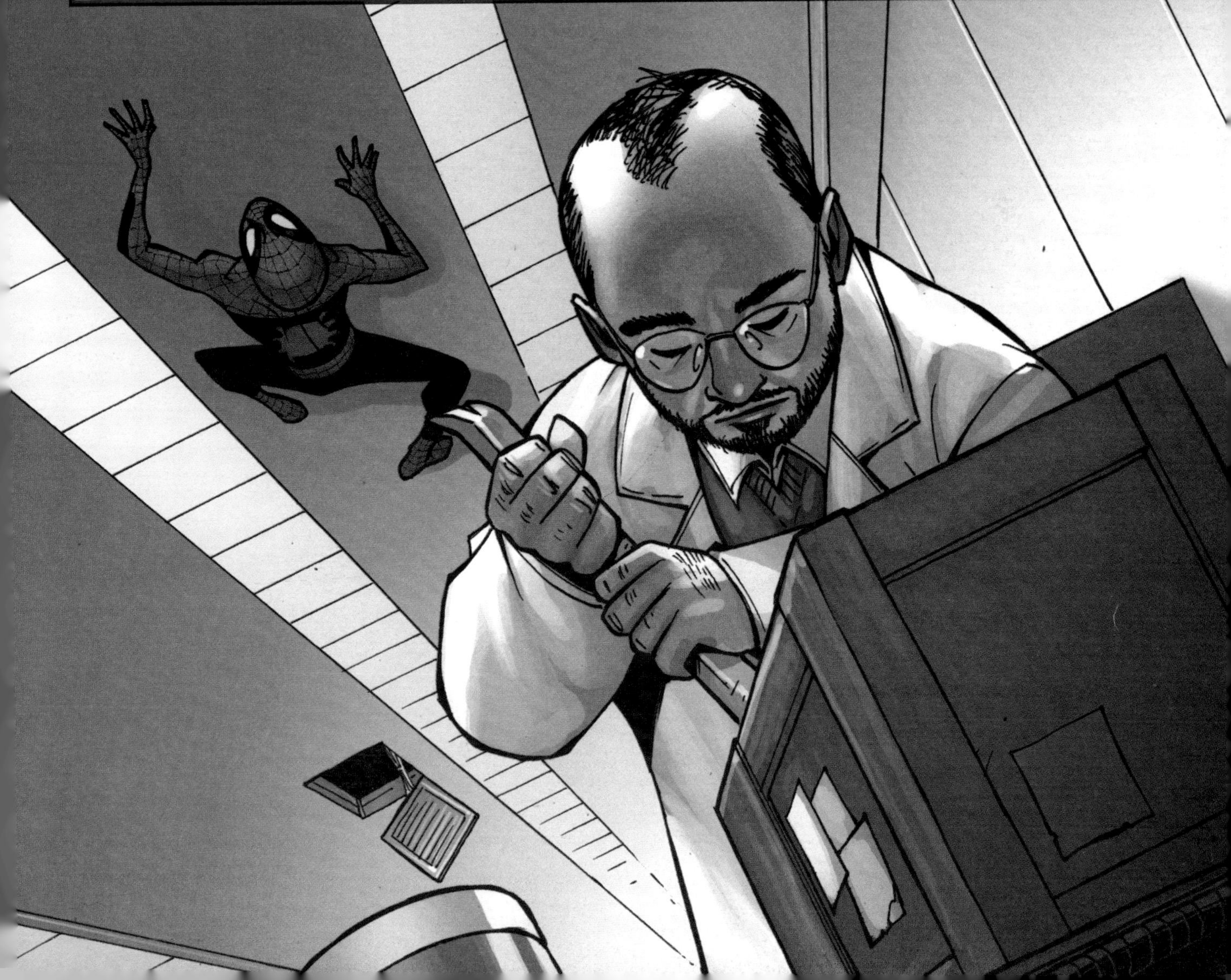

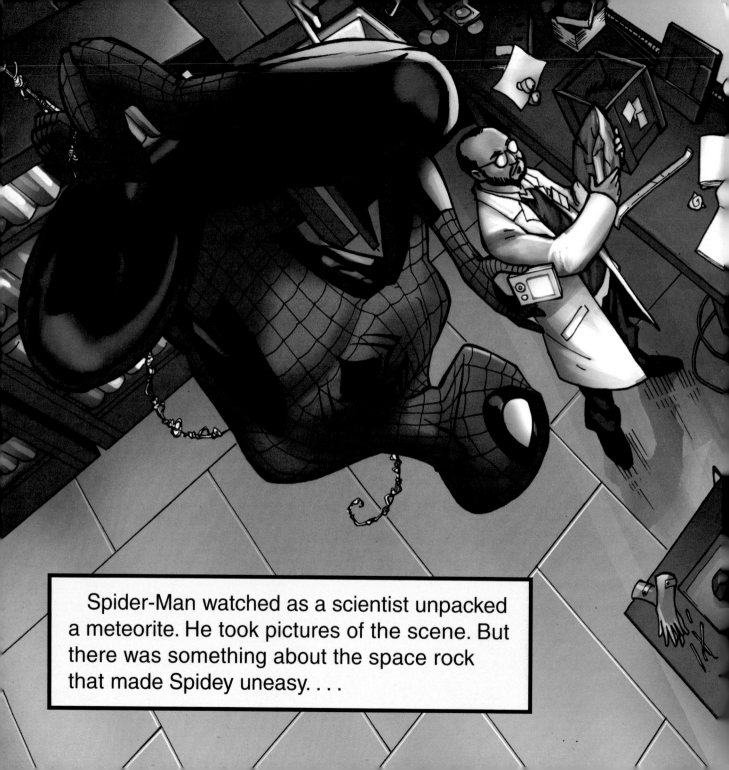

Spider-Man watched as a scientist unpacked a meteorite. He took pictures of the scene. But there was something about the space rock that made Spidey uneasy. . . .

The lab seemed strangely warm.
His spider-sense began to tingle.

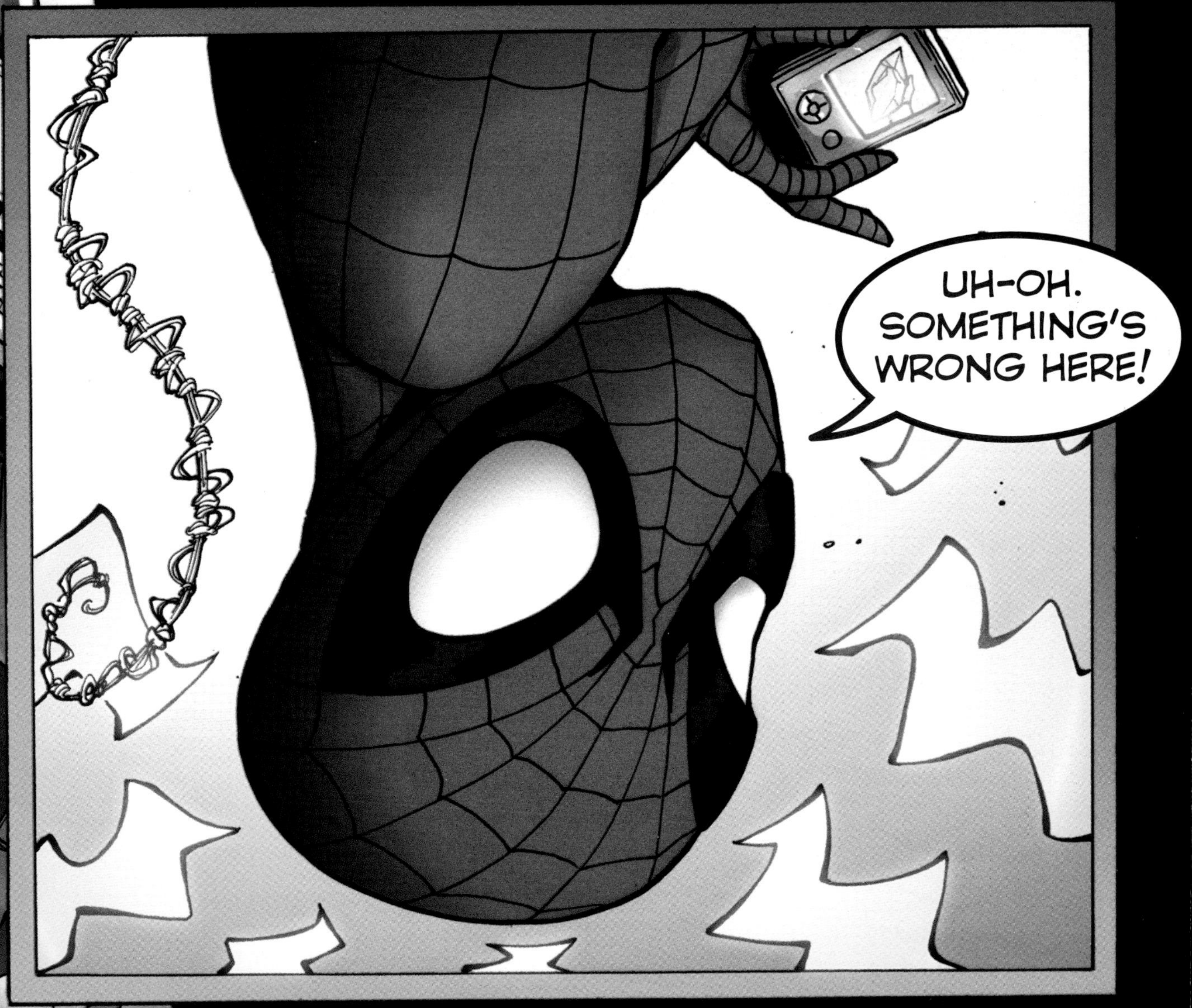
UH-OH. SOMETHING'S WRONG HERE!

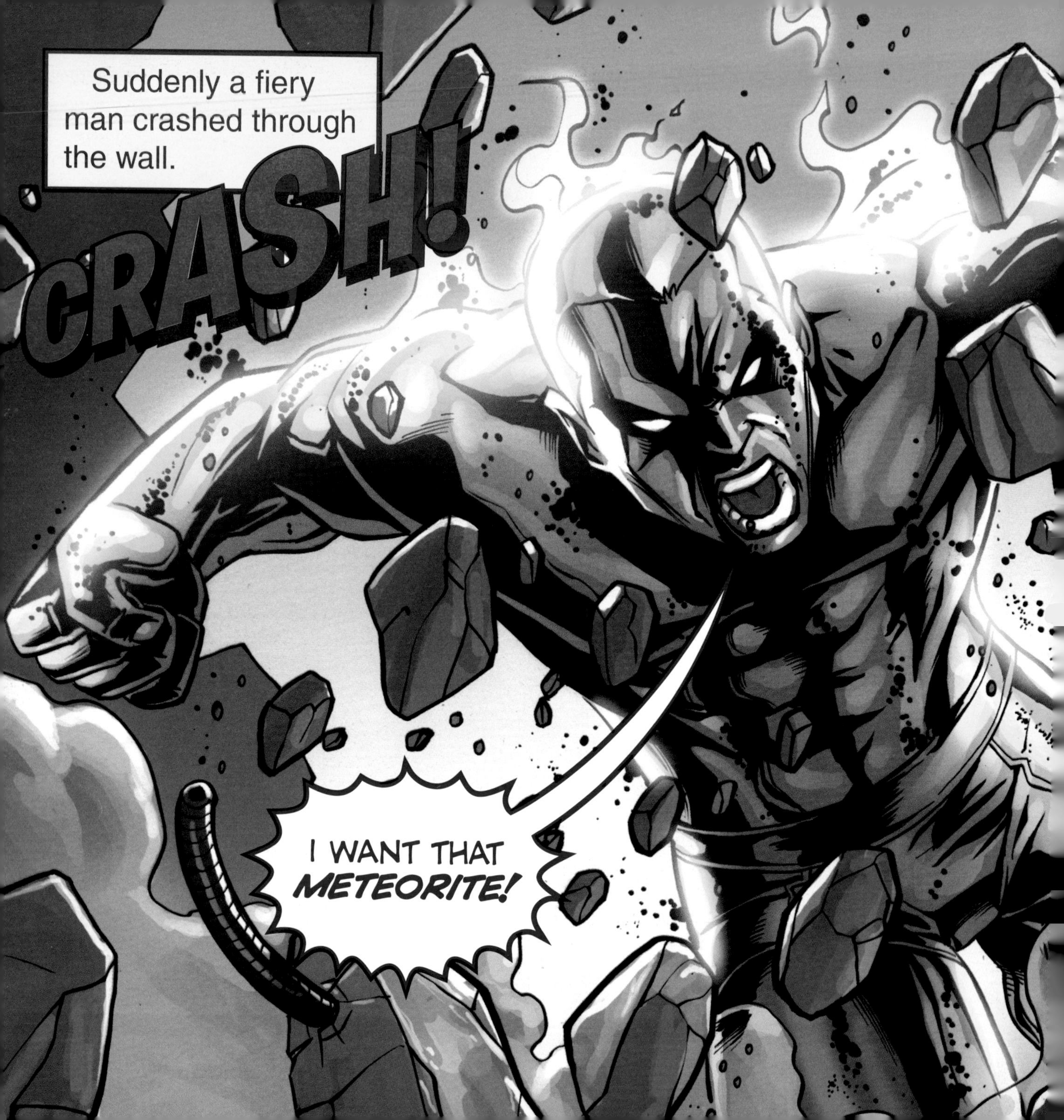
Suddenly a fiery man crashed through the wall.
CRASH!
I WANT THAT *METEORITE!*

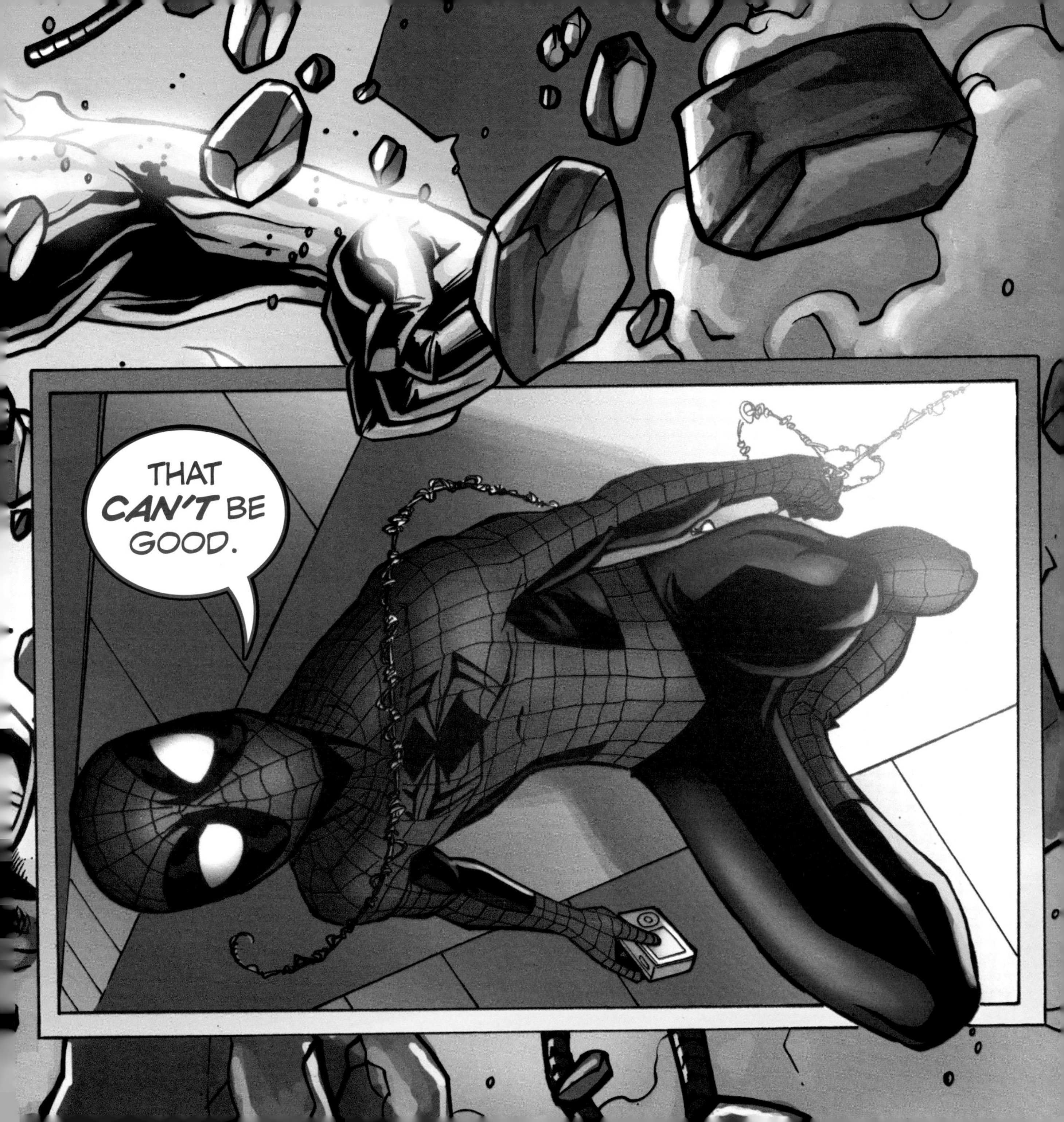
THAT CAN'T BE GOOD.

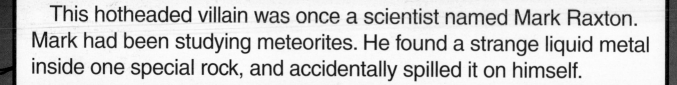

This hotheaded villain was once a scientist named Mark Raxton. Mark had been studying meteorites. He found a strange liquid metal inside one special rock, and accidentally spilled it on himself.

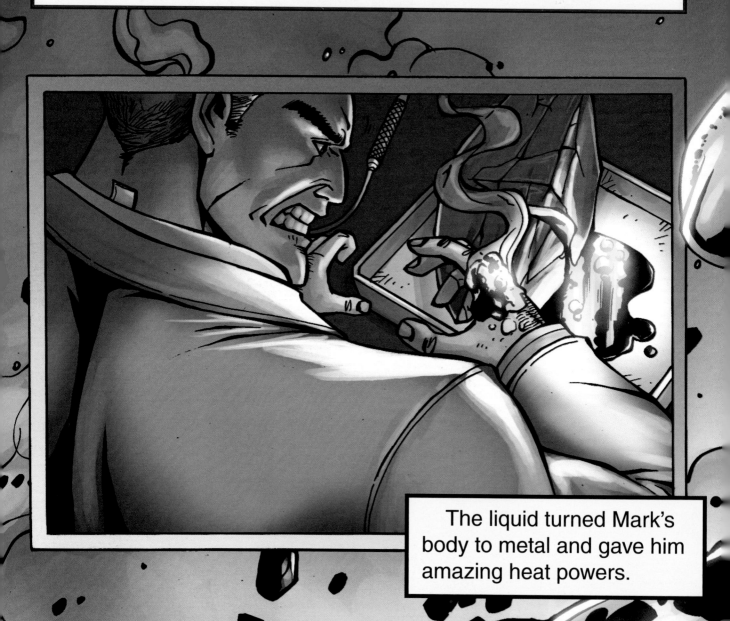

The liquid turned Mark's body to metal and gave him amazing heat powers.

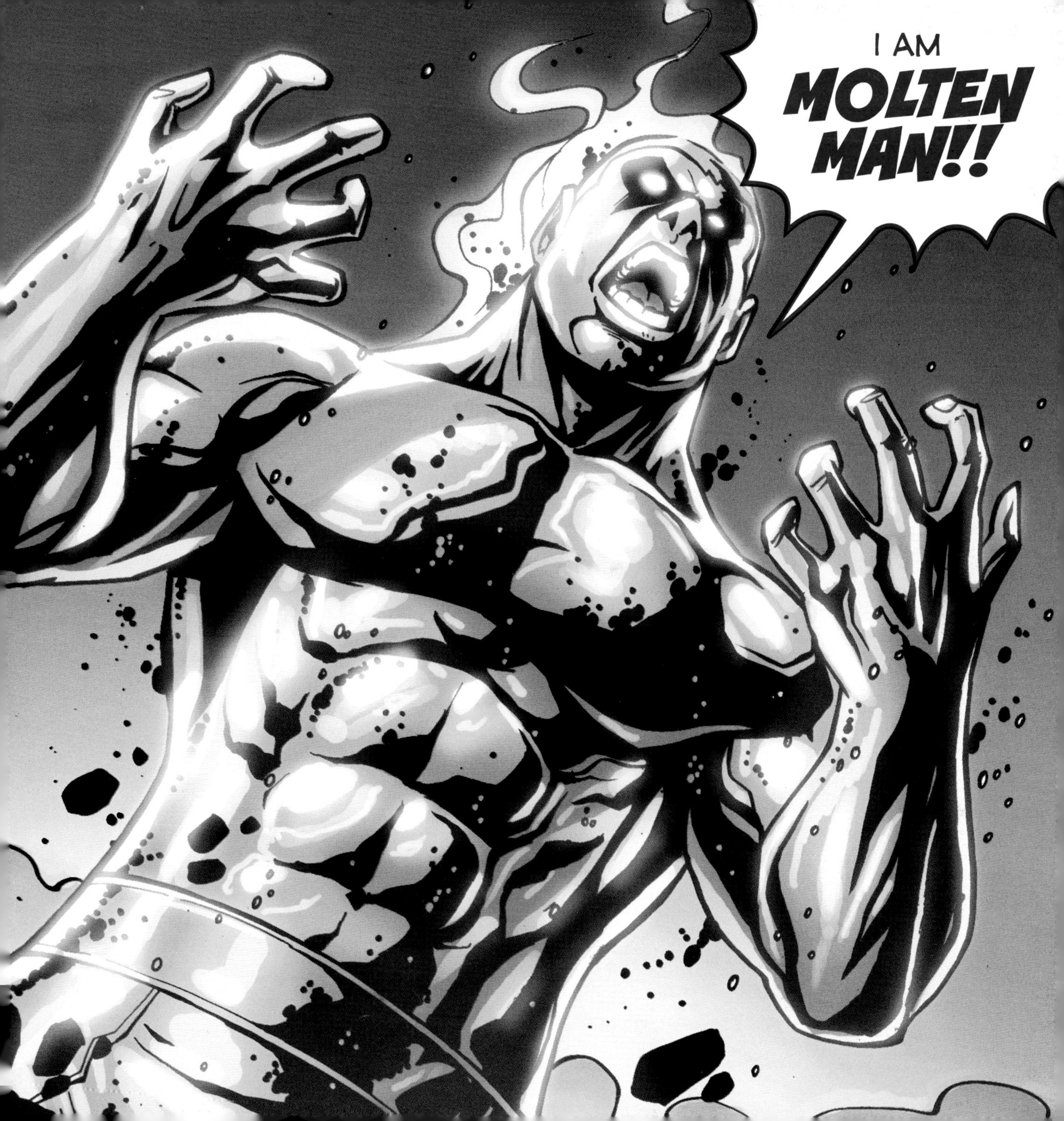
I AM MOLTEN MAN!!

Molten Man was now back to steal another chunk of the meteorite to make himself even stronger.

Spider-Man burst out of hiding to face his new foe. He tried to wrap up Molten Man in a cocoon of webbing.

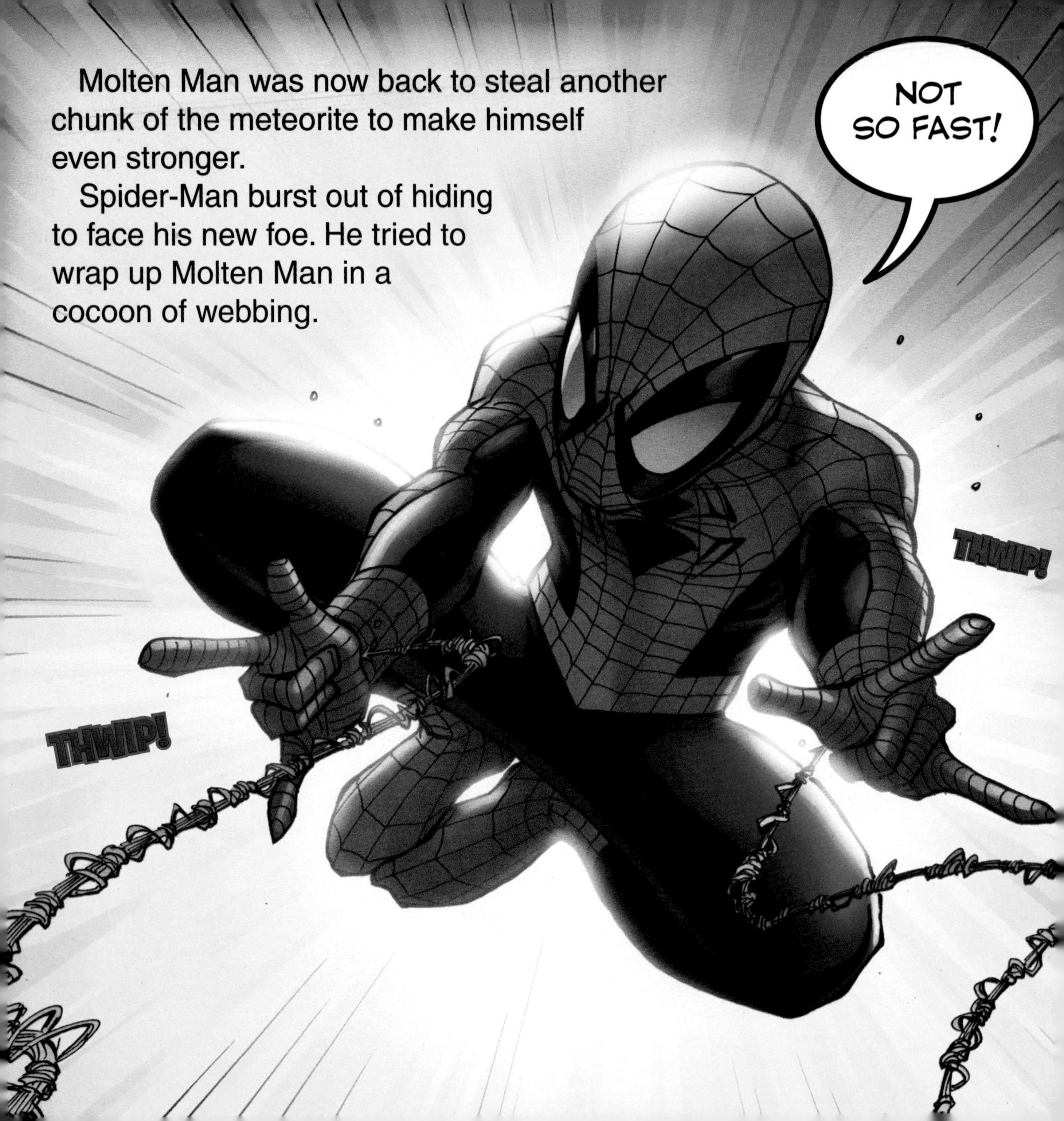
NOT SO FAST!
THWIP!
THWIP!

But the webs melted right off him!

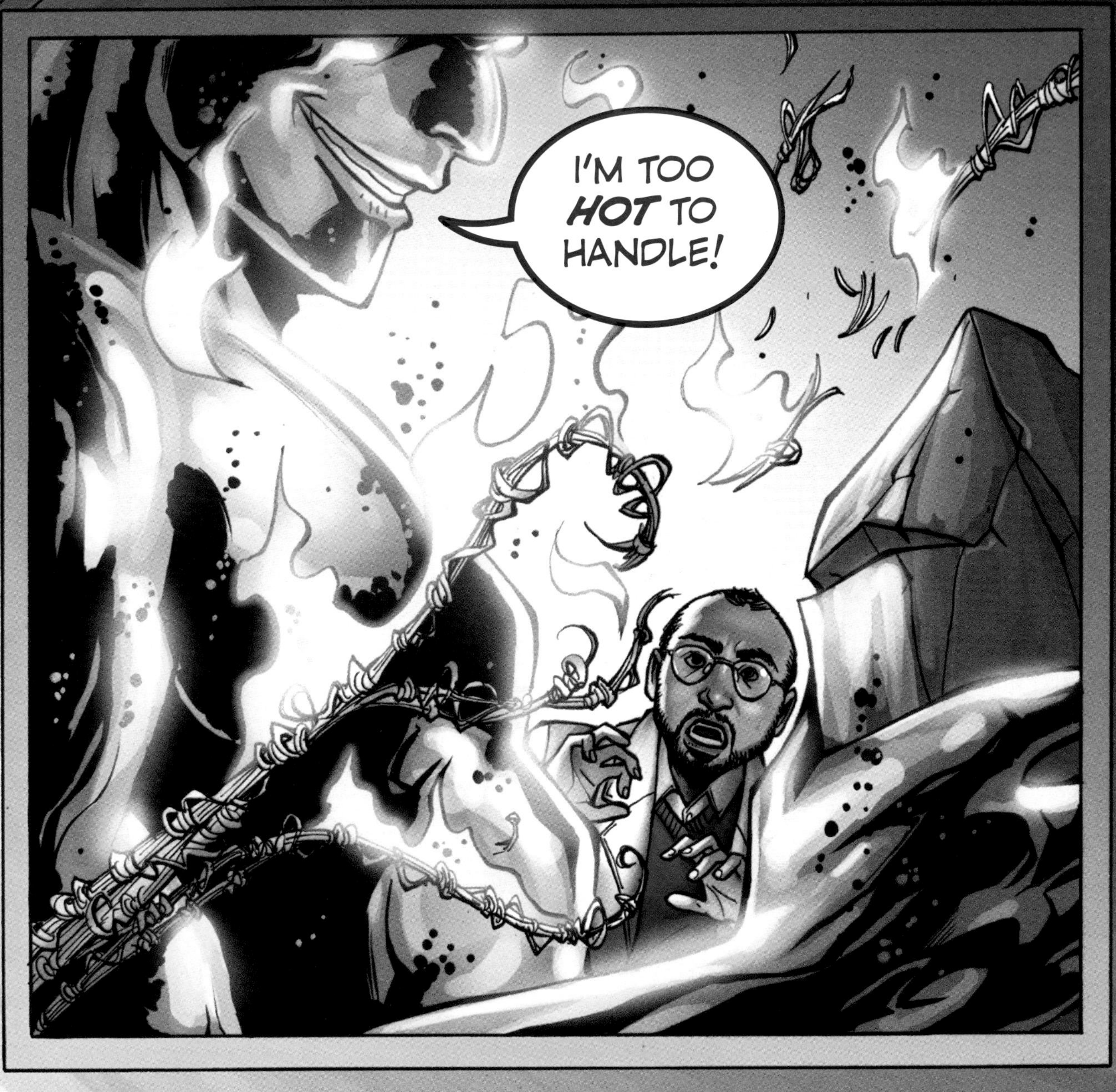
I'M TOO *HOT* TO HANDLE!

Spidey needed a new plan!
He hit the meteorite with a stream of webbing and pulled it away from Molten Man.

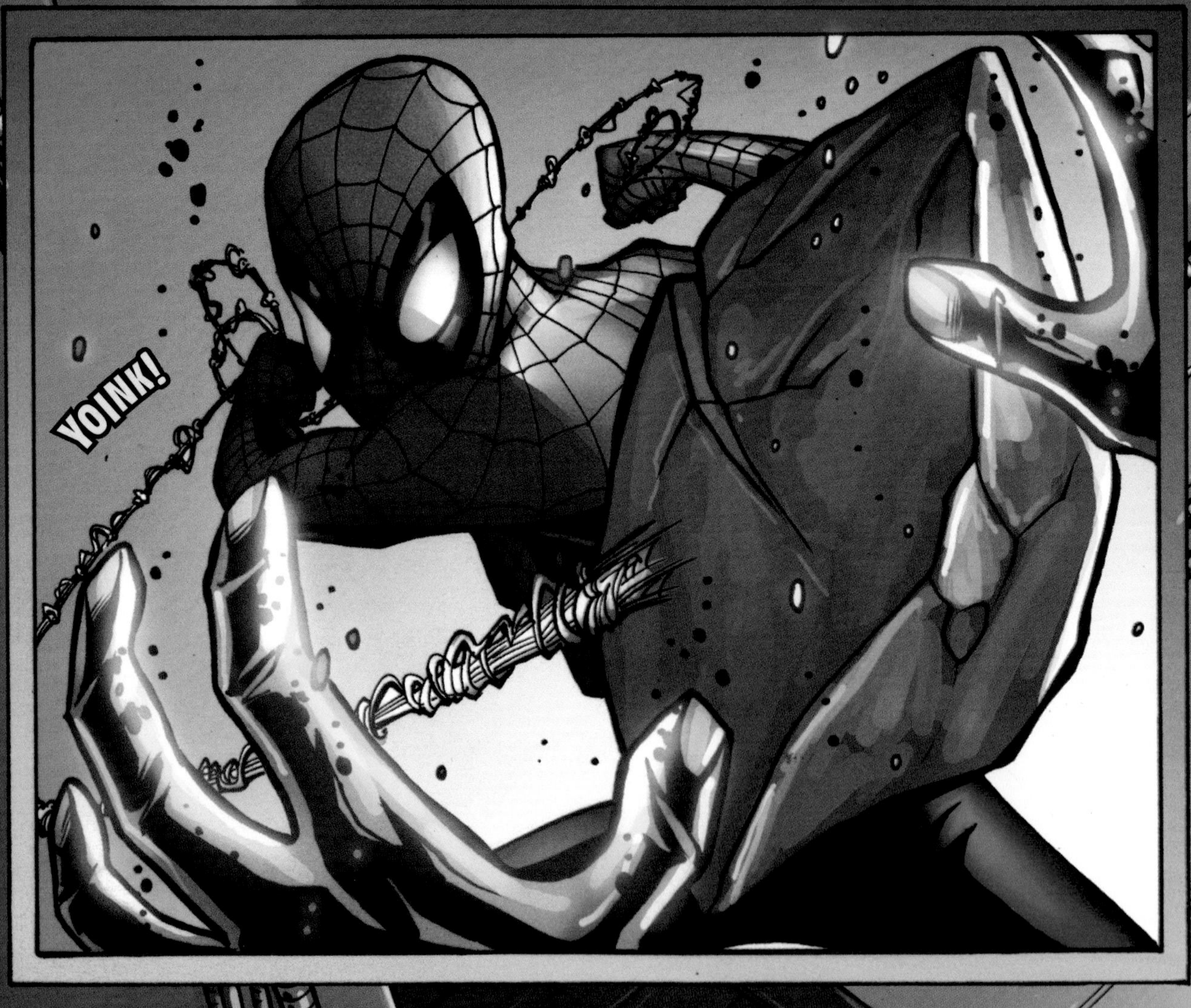
YOINK!

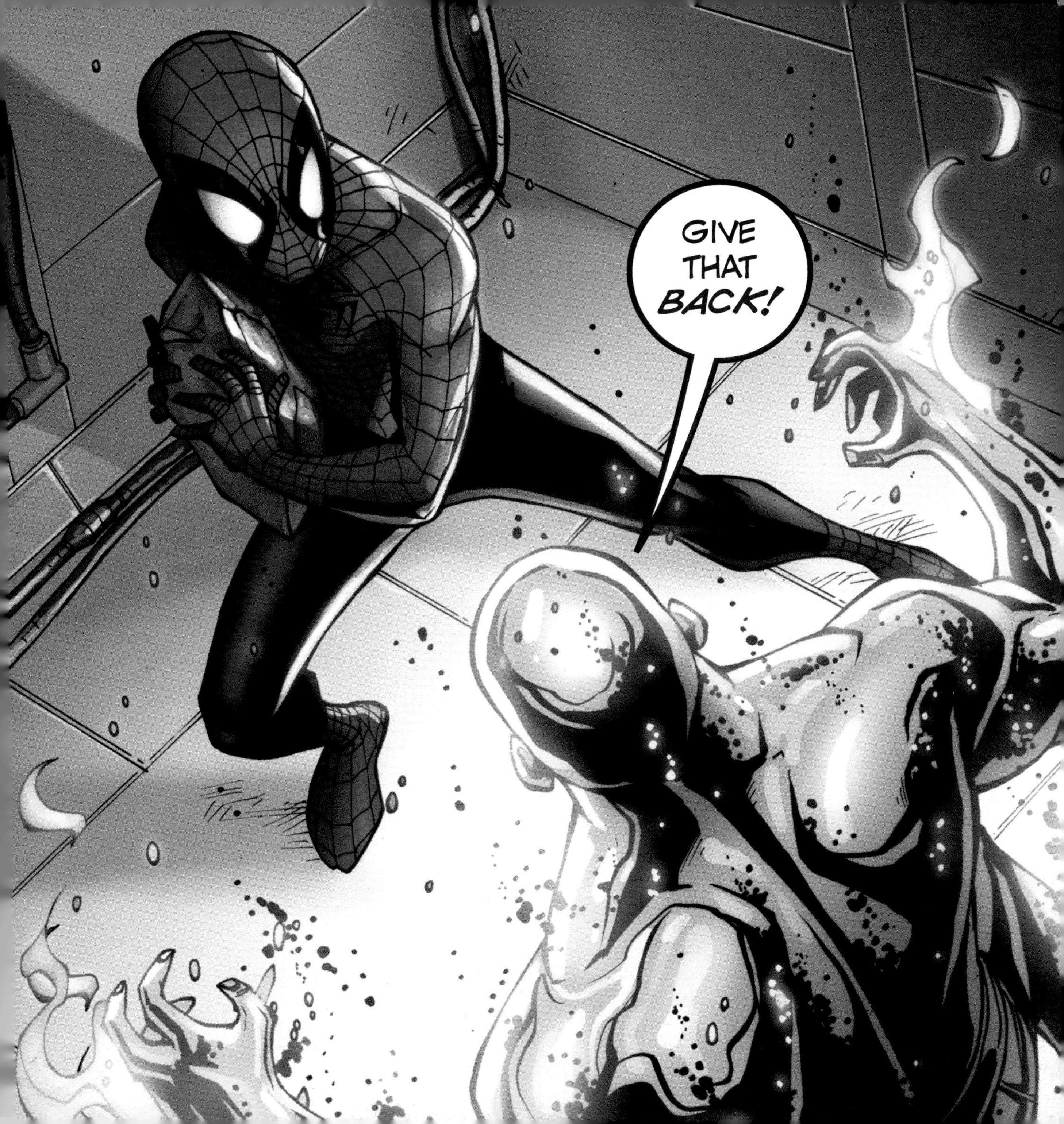
GIVE THAT BACK!

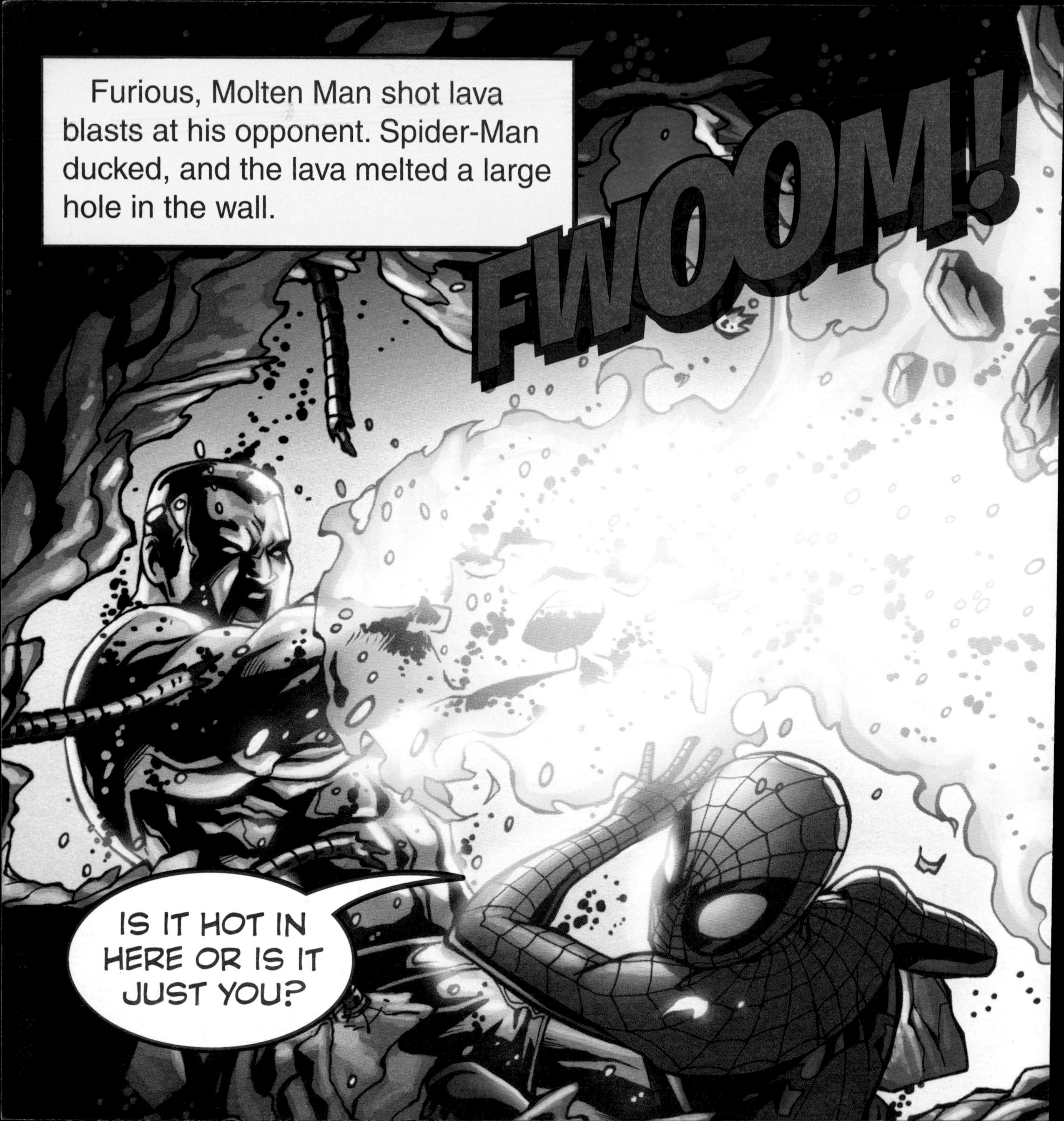
Furious, Molten Man shot lava blasts at his opponent. Spider-Man ducked, and the lava melted a large hole in the wall.
FWOOOM!
IS IT HOT IN HERE OR IS IT JUST YOU?

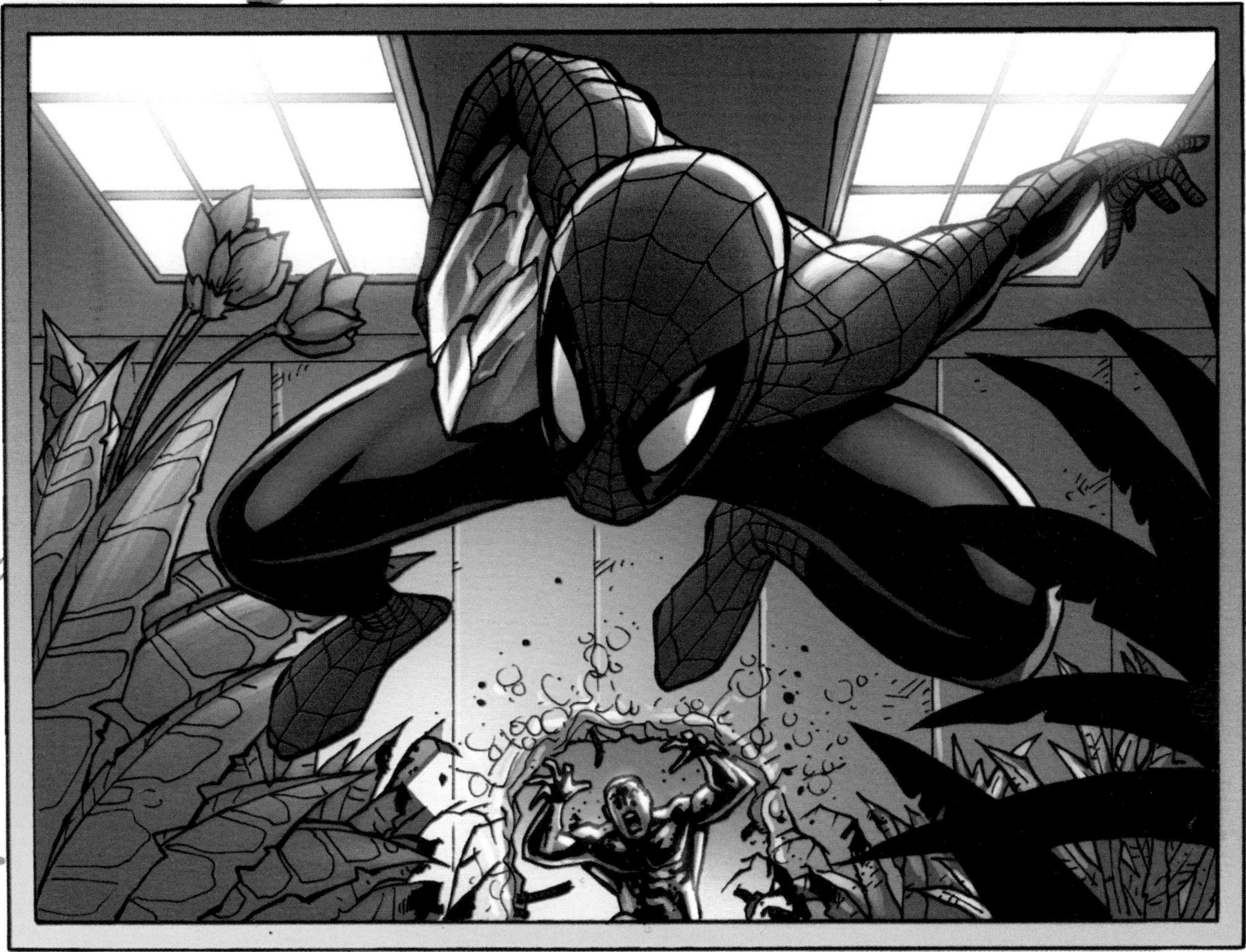

That gave Spider-Man an idea. Holding the meteorite, he jumped through the hole in the wall and landed in the hothouse.

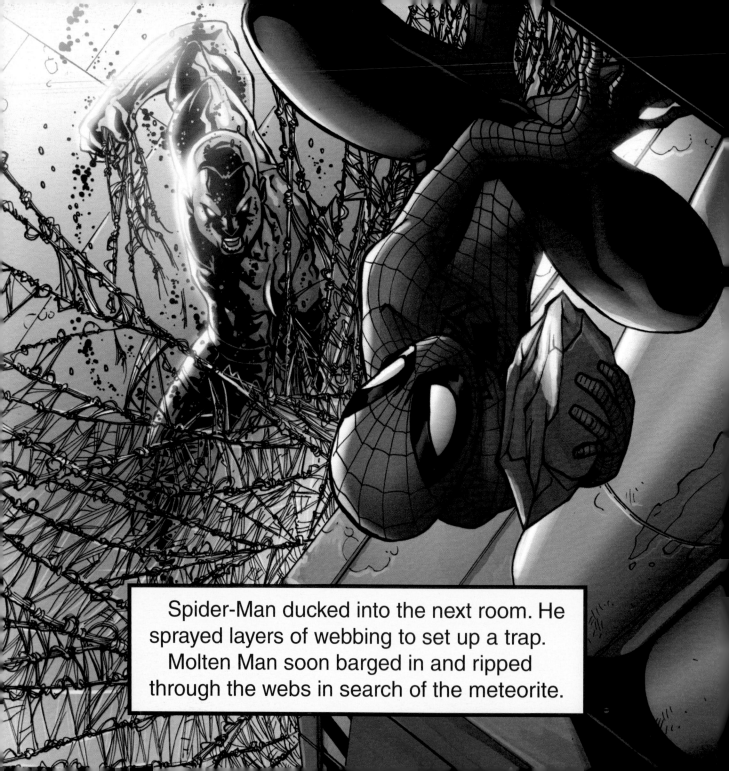

Spider-Man ducked into the next room. He sprayed layers of webbing to set up a trap. Molten Man soon barged in and ripped through the webs in search of the meteorite.

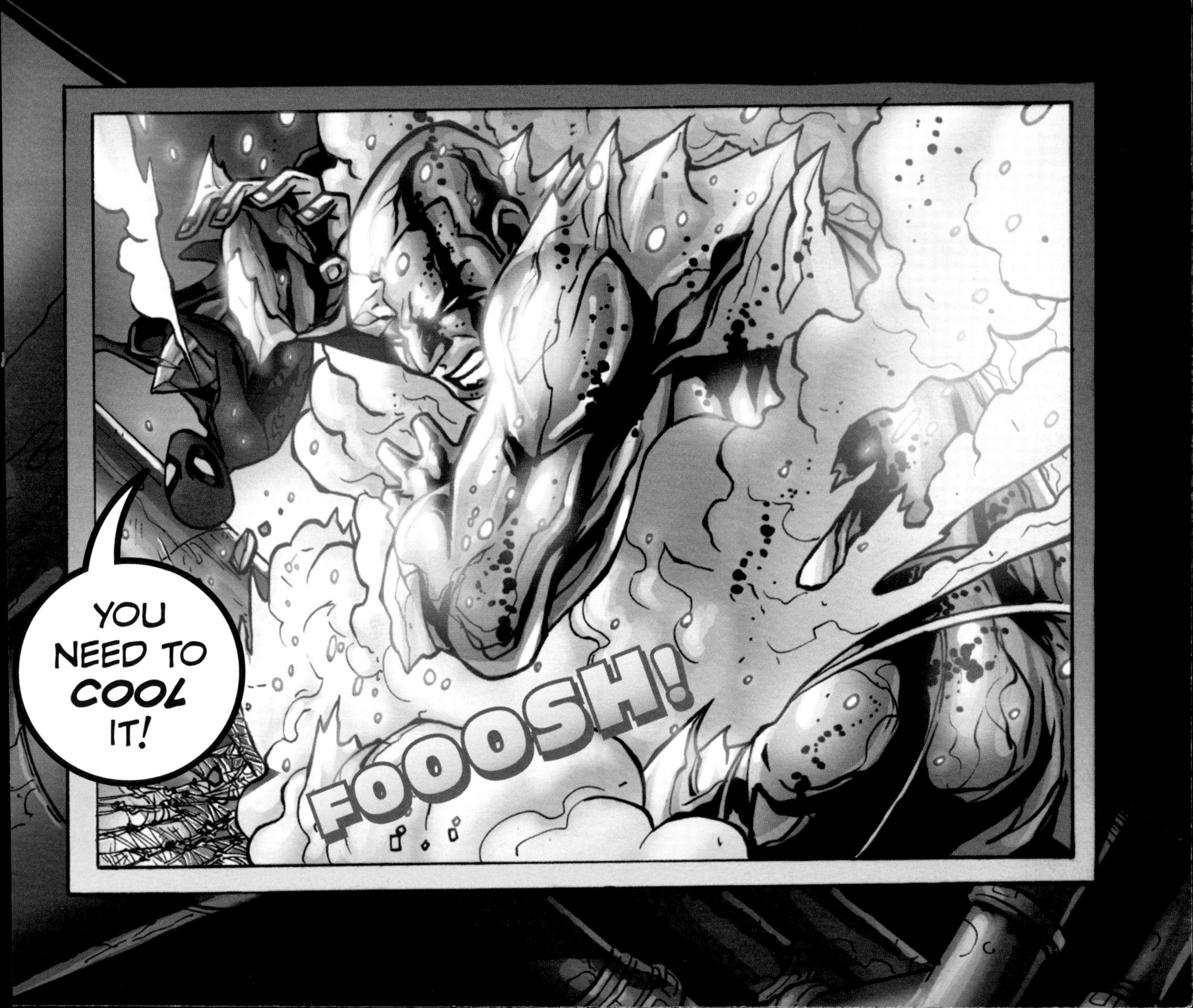
YOU NEED TO COOL IT!
FOOOSH!

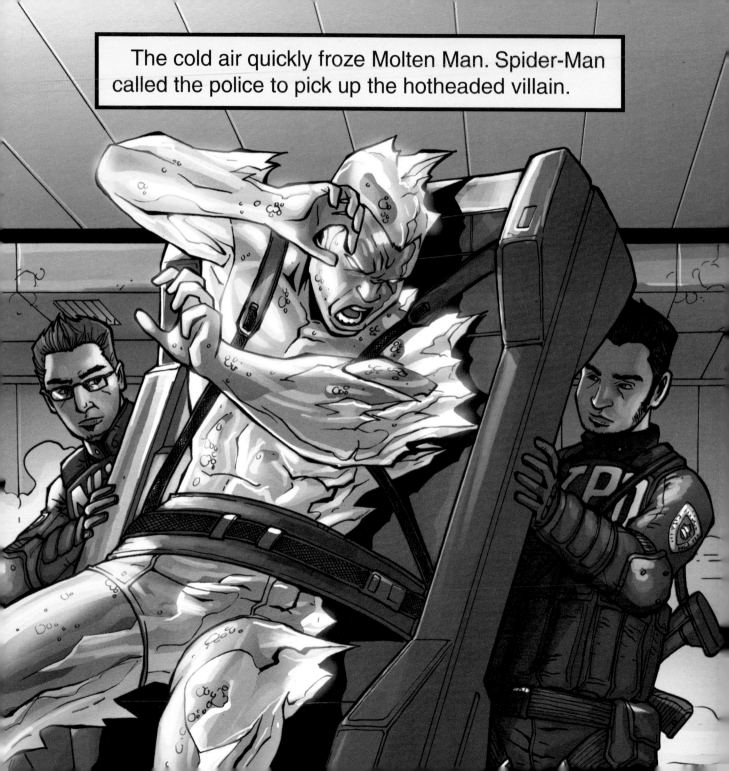

The cold air quickly froze Molten Man. Spider-Man called the police to pick up the hotheaded villain.

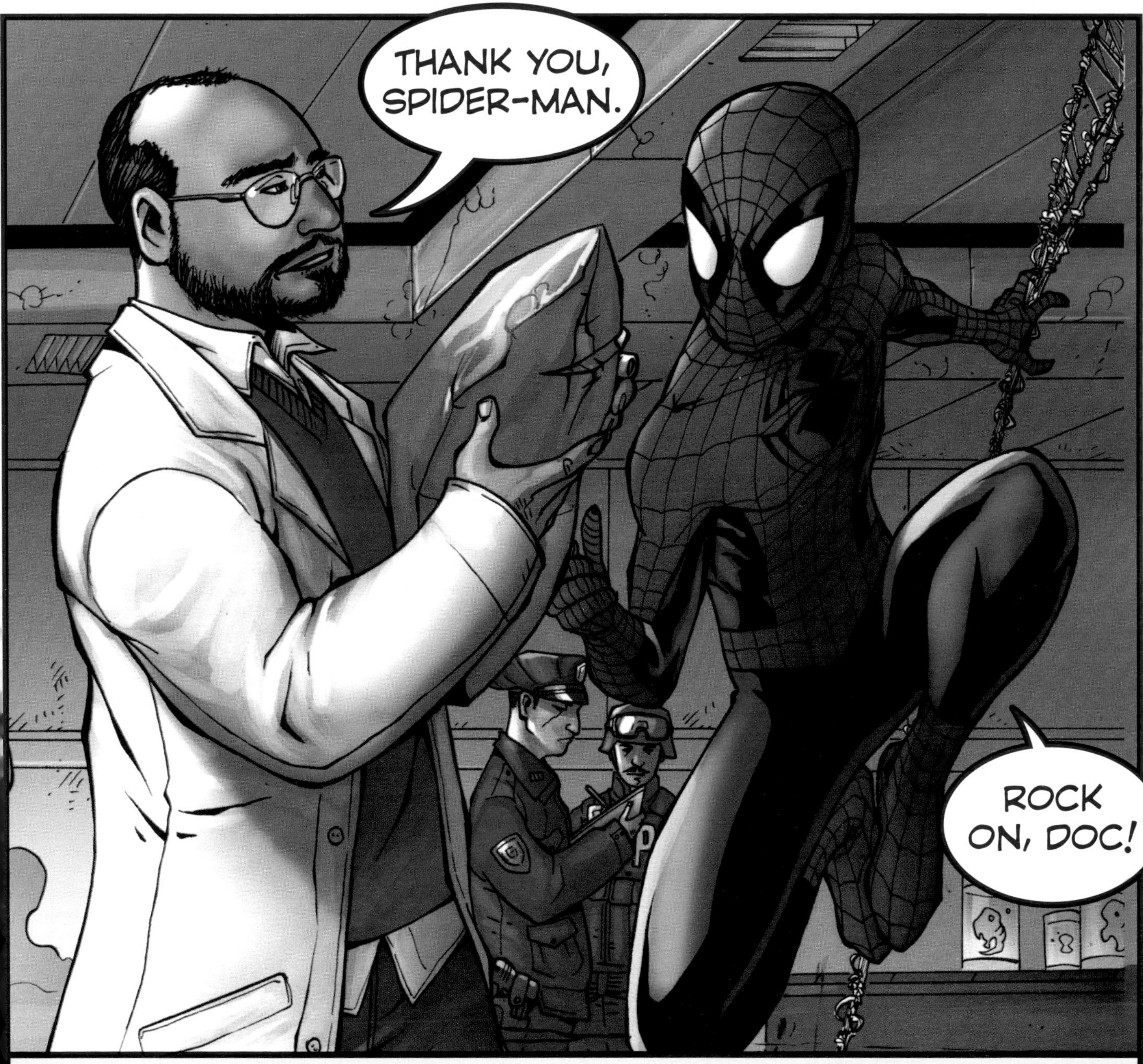
THANK YOU, SPIDER-MAN.
ROCK ON, DOC!

Then Spider-Man returned the meteorite to the grateful university scientist.

Peter was happy. He had done his job for Jameson, *and* he had stopped Molten Man!

Jameson was angry that Peter had not photographed the fight between Spider-Man and Molten Man.

Some days, Peter Parker just couldn't win.

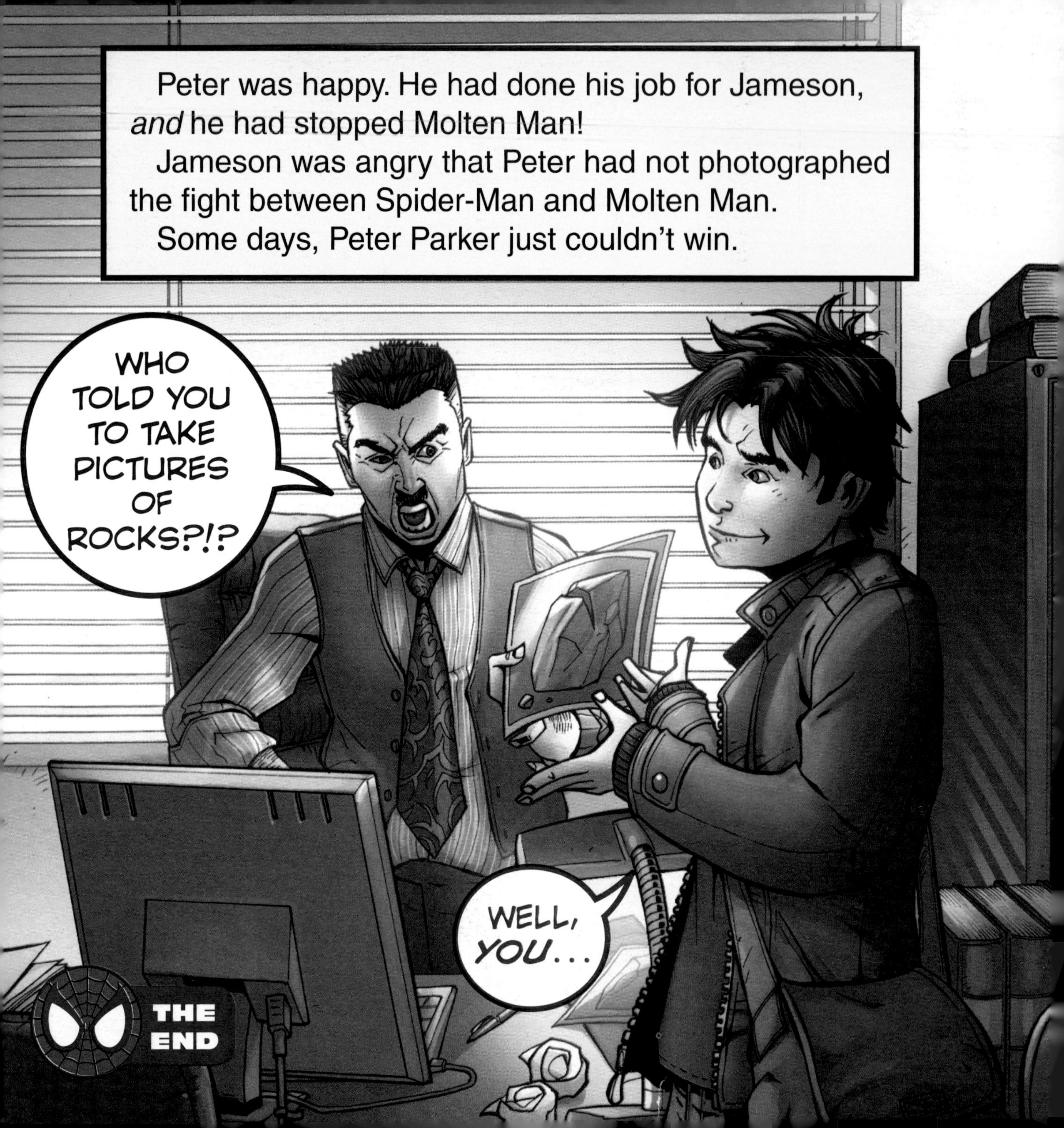
WHO TOLD YOU TO TAKE PICTURES OF ROCKS?!?
WELL, *YOU*...
THE END